Becoming a Kid

Learn to Earn

a Here's How You Can Too! adventure

ISBN: 978-1-0828-5163-6

Author: Amanda Yates

Illustrator: Lingxiao Guan

Published 2019

by Inspire Generations

hereshowyoucantoo.com

To Jonathan

insp\re
genera\ions

Inspire Generations (IG) is a social enterprise focussed on developing children's practical life skills. IG's belief is that if it can inspire one generation, they will go on to inspire another. IG donates at least 10% of its profits plus its content to education orientated charities, NGOs, bursaries and scholarships.

www.inspiregenerations.info

Chapter 1

No Money for Delicious Ice Cream

It's a warm Monday afternoon and the kids are at the local park where they often meet. After what felt like a long day at school they relax, discussing what happened on the weekend.

Good friends, Asmita and Mei are talking about the giant shopping spree that

Asmita's Mom took her on, and all the new dresses she bought. Alice's big brother Matt is pushing her on the swing. Her blonde pigtails are fluttering in the wind as they see how high he can get her to fly.

When suddenly a sound floats across the park, it is a familiar chiming sound coming from a van's speakers. Getting louder, as the van gets closer, the kids recognize the melody, an ice cream van. But not just any ice cream van, it's Jake's Grandfather's van, which is one of the most spectacular ice cream vans ever and known by all the locals. It is pink and white on the sides with a giant cone and massive swirly ice cream on top. But what makes it really stand out is the cheeky polar bear peeking over the cone on the roof. As the van comes to a halt, all the kids excitedly run over.

Jake runs up first and his Grandfather passes him his favorite, a yummy vanilla ice cream with chocolate topping covered in colorful sprinkles. Asmita, Mei and Lucy create a line excitedly, waiting to purchase their ice creams, but Leo and Kemba stand back. Neither boy has any money to buy ice cream.

Noticing that some of the kids don't have any money Jake's Grandfather climbs out of the van before selling any with an idea. He asks Jake to help round up the kids and sit on the grass with him.

Arranged on the grass in a circle, the kids are excited to hear what Jake's Grandfather has to say. Some of the parents are also interested too and are listening on in the background. Having been a businessman and an entrepreneur throughout his working life he decides to suggest his idea to the kids. "Hey kids I've got an idea, but before I tell you, does anyone know what an entrepreneur is?" Grandpa asks.

"I think so," Lucy says hesitantly.

While the rest of the kids all answer, "no," at the same time.

"What do you think it is Lucy?" Grandpa asks.

"A business owner?" Lucy replies questioningly.

"Yes, very close," Grandpa answers, "It's someone who sets up a business and works hard to make it successful. I've set up lots of businesses in my life, but my favorite is the ice cream van as I get to make kids like you happy every day."

"I love that you have the ice cream van too Grandpa," Jake says, licking his ice cream.

"I've been thinking about that Jake," Grandpa says, "not all the kids are as lucky as you. How about a friendly neighborhood challenge, to help everyone be able to afford little treats in life, like ice cream!"

"What kind of challenge?" Kemba asks, as one of the older kids he is interested to hear about any ways to make money. He would love to buy some new basketball shoes and has been saving his pocket money and birthday money for a while now but is yet to save enough.

"How about you try starting your own businesses and become Kid Entrepreneurs, just like I was a long, long, long time ago," Grandpa says with a chuckle. "I'll help you and provide tips along the way. That way you can learn what it takes to start a business and with summer vacation coming up, you will have money for all the things you want to do or buy. You might even be able to save for something bigger if your business is very successful."

"That's a great idea," Lucy says. The kids agree and nod. In fact, Matt's mind has already wondered off into a daydream about all the ice creams he could buy.

"When do we start?" Leo asks Grandpa, eager to get thinking about what business to start.

"How about right away? Think of a business that you can start and bring to the park on Sunday," Grandpa says, "we can advertise the event and have people come to spend their money, like a market day. I will come to the park at the same time every afternoon until then to answer any questions you have and offer lots of tips and tricks to make it easier for you."

"Yay!" the kids shout, jumping up from the grass, all chattering and excited about their plans for their new businesses.

Chapter 2

Try Something that has Worked Before

Sitting at the dinner table that night, Matt and Alice have their heads together talking about what kind of business they will start. "Yeah that's it!" Matt exclaims, accidentally spilling some of his spaghetti and meatballs.

"What are you two up to?" their Mom asks, "you've spilled your dinner Matt, please be more careful."

"Okay Mom, sorry," Matt says, "but we've chosen our business."

"Yeah, we're ent ent prenuurs," Alice says stumbling on the big word.

"Do you mean entrepreneurs Alice?" Mom asks.

"Yeah that's it," Alice replies animatedly.

"Are you talking about Jake's Grandfather's challenge?" Mom questions, "what have you decided to do?"

"We're going to hold a garage sale but at the park. We have heaps of stuff we don't really play with anymore," Matt says.

"Like your cousins Billy and Jane did? What a great idea kids, they made quite a lot of money selling their old toys," Mom replies.

"Yeah!" Matt exclaims, "I'm going to buy so many ice creams," Matt says, dreaming of all the flavors he will be able to buy with the money he makes from his new

business.

"I am sure that Dad and I will be able to

find things to add to your store as well. I'm

very impressed that you have come up

with such a great idea. We'll help you get

ready for Sunday," Mom says proudly.

Later that evening Matt walks past the

door to Alice's bedroom and sees her

sitting on the floor. She has craft all around

her, there is cardboard and glue, scissors

and coloring pens. "What are you making

Alice?" Matt questions.

"A card for Mom's birthday," Alice shows

Matt the almost finished card, with colored

cardboard balloons stuck to the front.

"How do you know how to make cards?"

Matt asks.

"I learned at preschool!" Alice replies

proudly.

"Wow!" Matt exclaims, "you could make more and sell them at our store on Sunday."

"You think?" Alice asks, "okay but I don't know how to write the words, can I leave them blank?"

Chapter 3

Teaming Up with a Friend

It's lunchtime at school on Tuesday, Kemba and Leo have been playing basketball with their friends. Puffed out, after a big game they sit down on the side of the court to eat their lunch and start talking about their plans for their businesses.

"What business are you going to start

Leo?" Kemba asks.

"You know how much I love my dog Oreo,"

Leo says whole-heartedly, "I think that I

will start a dog walking service.

I already take Oreo for walks. I can take other dogs too."

"Oh cool," Kemba exclaims, "that's perfect for you and there are lots of people around that don't have time to walk their dogs, so you can help!"

"Yeah, I'm really excited about it," Leo says, "what are you going to do?"

"I want to try to make the most money but also have fun too, of course. I've decided to do a car wash. It doesn't cost a lot to start up, I just need some buckets, sponges, soap and water. I'm sure there will be lots of people at the park with dirty cars," Kemba replies thinking that he has thought of the perfect business to run.

"You know there is a tap at the park, right by the road," Leo reminds Kemba supportively, "and you can get the adults to drive their cars to that spot. I can work in your car wash with you if you want help," Leo offers.

"What about your business?" Kemba asks, quietly hoping that Leo will be able to help him because washing cars by himself won't be much fun without a friend.

"I'm planning to advertise my business and take bookings for weekends and after school so I will be free to wash cars in between," Leo replies.

"Perfect, with you helping we will be able to wash loads more cars," Kemba says

enthusiastically, dollar signs sparkling in
his eyes.

Chapter 4

Preparation is Crucial for Success

The kids and their parents have all come back to the park to see Jake's Grandfather to discuss their plans for their businesses. He wants to see if there are any tips he can share to give them the best chance of success. They are also working on the advertisements for their market day because unless people know it's happening the market won't be very busy.

The kids are spread out on the grass under

the shade trees making the signs and

flyers they will use to advertise. They have

cardboard and colorful paints to make the

signs to hang around the park, as well as

the town. While they are working hard

Grandpa wanders around talking to each

of the kids to see how their plans are

progressing.

"Leo, I can see that you are drawing a dog on this sign, have you decided what your business will be?" Grandpa asks.

"Yes, I'm going to be a dog walker," Leo replies decidedly.

"That's a great business for you," Grandpa responds, "I've met your dog Oreo and you are a very responsible pet owner. Have you given any thought about other services you can offer, other than dog walking?"

"No, I haven't," Leo replies interested in what Grandpa's suggestion will be.

"Check with your parents first, but you could offer pet sitting as well, for an extra fee of course," Grandpa suggests, "that way your customers will know their pets will be well looked after when they go away on holidays."

"That's a great idea," Leo says appreciatively, already imagining how many extra customers this will give him.

"Thanks for the idea."

Next Grandpa heads over to Mei who is working on her laptop to create the market day advertising flyers with Asmita and Lucy, "How are the flyers coming along Mei?" Grandpa asks.

"I'm stuck. What do they need to say besides the time and date of the market?" Mei questions.

"Well, they need to have all the important information to tell the customers about the event," Grandpa replies, "Let's include what stores will be here and any other services, like Kemba's carwash as this will make it more appealing to customers."

"Okay," the girls chorus. They continue to make sure the flyers have all the correct information, as well as being bright and colorful to get customers attention.

"That looks great kids," Grandpa exclaims, looking at the giant letters, M A R K E T, that Jake, Matt and Alice have been painting on the back of some old cardboard boxes. They are copying the letters that Grandpa wrote for them.

"We're going to hang it on the park fence over there," Jake says pointing in the direction.

"People won't be able to miss the signs with all the bright colors you've used,"

Grandpa replies, "instead of over there," referring to the spot that Jake pointed to, "I think you should hang it up on the busy roadside of the park, that way more customers will be able to see the signs. Have you decided what business you are going to start yet Jake?" His Grandpa asks.

"No, not yet," Jake replies, "I'm still thinking."

"That's ok Jake," Grandpa assures, "there is still plenty of time. He then turns to Alice and Matt. "I'm thrilled to hear of your garage sale, what a great idea. Your Mom tells me that they are going to provide some items to sell too. Just remember that people love a bargain, so don't be greedy setting your prices too high and you should attract more customers."

"Ok, I'll try to remember that," Alice says.

"Good tip," Matt agrees.

"We've finished the flyers," Asmita calls out.

"Oh good," Grandpa says as he walks back over to the girls, "here's some change to get them printed at the library. You can hand them out the flyers and stick the posters up there, as well as at the shops."

"I'll go past the dog park on my way home,

I can take some there too," Lucy offers.

Chapter 5

Earn Money Doing Something You Love

During lunchtime at school, Jake and Matt are playing with Jake's magic set under a big shady tree after eating their sandwiches. Matt has been telling Jake about the garage sale that he is setting up with Alice on Sunday. They have been talking about all the toys that Matt and Alice have decided they don't want

anymore and are going to sell in their

store.

"What are you going to do on Sunday Jake?" Matt asks. "You know how much I love magic," Jake replies happily, "I'm going to do a magic show. I could sell tickets or maybe ... leave a hat out for tips."

"Like musicians do at the train station? What a good idea," Matt exclaims, "you're getting really good at tricks."

"And I have a new magicians cape and top hat," Jake says excitedly, "want to help me practice my tricks?"

Chapter 6

Thinking About Others

After school, Lucy and Mei have come to Asmita's house and are looking at how full her wardrobe is after her weekend shopping spree. Her wardrobe is a mess and the clothes are almost falling out.

"I can't fit any more clothes in," Asmita

says trying to hang her new purple dress

in the wardrobe.

"Yeah, it's so full," Lucy agrees, picking up another dress that needs to be hung and handing it to Asmita.

"Some clothes don't even fit me anymore," Asmita says flicking a frilly pink dress, "but I don't know what to do with it all."

"Why don't you start a clothes store for the market day?" Mei suggests after looking at the clothes and noticing that they are all in very good condition.

"That's a super idea," Asmita says, "That way, I'll have more space in my wardrobe, and I will have some money to go shopping again!" She says with a chuckle.

"Any clothes you don't sell you could donate them to a charity," Lucy suggests, thinking of the yearly clean out she does with her Mom.

"Yes," Asmita and Mei agree, "wonderful idea."

"That's my business sorted," Asmita says,
"what have you two decided to do?"

"I spoke to my Mom last night," Mei says
"and she is going to help me set up a store.
I'm going to sell some of the crafts from
her shop and also others that I have made
myself. It'll be great practice for the school
holidays as I'm going to help her in the
shop."

"Oh cool! Lucy, what are you doing?"
Asmita asks.

"I'm going to start a photography service with the new camera that I got for my birthday," Lucy says, "I've been watching heaps of videos online to learn how to take stunning photos. I'll take photos at the market and customers can buy them from me if they like them."

"That's awesome!" Asmita exclaims, "are you going to take bookings for other events?"

"Yeah, you could take photos at birthday parties, or other events where there are lots of people," Mei suggests.

"I really like that idea," Lucy says, motivated about the opportunity to grow her photography service.

Chapter 7

Plan Ahead and Use a List

The next afternoon Asmita and her Mom are looking through her wardrobe deciding which clothes to include in her store. There are large piles of clothes that are too small for her on her bed, as well as some shoes, bags and other accessories in another pile on the floor.

"Mom, there is so much to do before Sunday," Asmita says worryingly.

"Well, one of the things I use to make sure that I have everything completed is a checklist," Asmita's Mom says, "I sit down and think of all the things I need to do, write a list and check it off as I go. That way I don't forget anything."

"That's an excellent idea, now that we have sorted through all the clothes, I can make my list," Asmita agrees.

Chapter 8

Final Checks

Friday afternoon rolls around quickly and now that the boys have all decided what they will do for the market. They have met up with Jake's Grandfather at the park. He's brought cardboard and paint in lots of bright colors for the boys to make the signs that will advertise their businesses. Jake has also collected some streamers and glitter from home to make his magic show signs.

"Do you like my sign?" Matt asks Grandpa lifting his garage sale sign high in the air.

"It's great," Grandpa says, "I like the big bold letters you have used."

Grandpa sees that Kemba is making a gigantic sign and comments on how big it is.

"Yeah, it's so that people driving past can see it no matter how fast they are going," Kemba says.

"Great idea," Grandpa replies, "hopefully they will pull over for a wash. You can also make another one with prices on it so the customers can choose what type of wash they want. How are you going to display it?"

"I'll tape it to the pole, so it doesn't blow away," Kemba states.

"Don't forget that you can also offer to clean the interiors of the cars too," Grandpa suggests. "Leo, what is going to be on your dog walking sign?"

"It'll say Leo's Dog Walking Service," Leo replies, "and I've made flyers to hand out as well, they have my price list and contact details."

Leo's Dog Walking Service

Phone Number: 0123456789
Email: leo@email.com

I walk well behaved dogs all around this neighbourhood. I have a medium sized dog myself but love all types of dogs. I am responsible and trustworthy.

Walk and play
30 minutes $_
60 minutes $_

Pet Sit
Weeknight overnight $_
Weekend 24 hours $_
Weekend 48 hours $_
School holidays per 24 hours $_

"That sounds great, why don't you add a

sentence about your experience with

dogs." Grandpa suggests, "you should definitely hand out a flyer to anyone who comes with a dog to the market, but it may be a bit of a lucky dip to know which people to talk to that have dogs at homes."

"How is your sign for your magic show coming along Jake?" Grandpa asks, "you sure have managed to get glitter everywhere, it's even in your hair!"

"I've just finished it," Jake says proudly, "and I made tickets to sell too."

Jake's Magic Show Ticket

Admits 1 person only

11th January 12:00pm $ —

"That's very good," Grandpa says looking

at the palm-sized, rectangular tickets,

"they have the name of your show, the

time and date, location and the price. And

they look great too, people may even want

to keep them as souvenirs."

Chapter 9

Important Business Decisions

Saturday morning has arrived and there's only one day to go. All the kids are making the final preparations for their stalls, services and shows. Matt and Alice are going through their toys one last time and deciding which ones they can truly part with. They are also checking with their Mom and Dad before making the price stickers for their items and packing them into the car to take to the park tomorrow.

"You kids have done a great job of cleaning up while deciding which toys to part with," Mom says, "and Alice your cards are lovely, you should be very proud of yourself."

"Thanks Mom," Alice says happily, as she packs up the stand to display her cards.

"Now that you have sorted out your toys, we should make a list recording the price for your items. It will help you to be super organized for when you are busy with customers," Mom suggests, "that will make sure there are no mistakes in case some of the price stickers come off." Agreeing, Matt jumps up to get a notepad and pen for Mom to start writing their list.

Kemba's Mom is also helping him to get ready for his car wash, they have gone shopping to buy the buckets, sponges and car washing liquid that he and Leo will need to wash the cars.

"Do you think we have everything you will need for tomorrow?" Mom asks Kemba.

"I think so," Kemba replies carrying shopping bags full of car washing supplies, "thank you for taking me shopping."

"That's okay Kemba," Mom says, "I'm very happy with how responsible you are being and using your own money to start your business. You know what your Grandpa always used to say..."

"Sometimes you need to spend money to make money," Kemba chants.

"Exactly, and because you have done such a great job organizing your car wash, I will be your first customer!" Mom says proudly.

Jake is also finalizing his show for tomorrow. Grandpa is helping him pack up all his stage equipment and his props. While packing they are talking about the plans for the market.

"Does it look like everyone will be ready for the big day tomorrow?" Grandpa asks Jake.

"I think so," Jake replies excitedly.

"The advertising campaign has gone very well, the lady at the library gave me a flyer this week," Grandpa says, "word around town is that you may all be very busy tomorrow, lots of people may come for a look."

"Yay," Jake exclaims, "do you think they will want to see my show?"

"I'm sure they will, your dad has been telling everyone at his coffee shop about your show and the market," Grandpa tells Jake.

"I better keep practicing these harder tricks then," Jake says, "will you help me practice Grandpa?"

"Of course I will. What else are Grandpas for!" Grandpa says with a smile.

Chapter 10

It's Market Day!

It is a warm and sunny day, not a cloud in the sky. The kids have all arrived at the park extra early to prepare their businesses. Their parents have all come to help too and are carting the heavier items like tables from their cars. The kids gather talking excitedly as they set up their stalls.

There is a buzz around the park, it's

market day.

Alice and Matt are running around

frantically trying to set up their garage

sale. They are dumping their stuff all over the tables and even on the ground. After Mom and Dad have brought over the last of the big items, they help Matt and Alice to order their items in a neat way that should help to attract customers. They have also made sure to price their sale items without being greedy because as Grandpa says, "customers love a bargain."

Grandpa has also brought his ice cream van to the market. He is hanging up balloons and playing music from his van to create the excitement of a party. As the market commences there is almost an immediate flock of people from the town who arrive and eagerly look around the shops. In the background, there is a line of three cars already waiting to be washed at Kemba's car wash. Lucy is walking around taking photos of the market and talking to customers. She stops to speak to Grandpa about the photos she has been taking and how her business is going.

"I'm so glad that I decorated this t-shirt to advertise my photography service," Lucy says to Grandpa as he reads her t-shirt,

Kid Photographer for Hire

"Yes, I have seen that you are stopping people to take their photo and talk about your service," Grandpa replies. "Have you taken many bookings?"

"Two birthday parties for kids from school," Lucy says happily.

As the day goes on Grandpa circles around

and speaks to each of the kids. He has

come over to where Asmita and Mei have

set up their stalls. Mei has a big yellow

umbrella shading her table of arts and crafts and has used the umbrella to display her hanging goods. Asmita has her used clothing store right next door with racks full of clothes, a portable change room to try clothes on and a big mirror. Grandpa has noticed that the girls have been helping each other with their customers and brings it up with Mei.

"Asmita has been helping me," Mei tells

Grandpa, "I've been very busy, all the

customers want to bargain with me on

price."

"Ah yes," Grandpa says sympathetically, "negotiation can be tricky, bargaining back and forth, as you don't want to lose the customer but also want to sell for the highest price. But you will get better at it, it just takes practice."

"I've been trying to help," Asmita says, "I can see how busy Mei has been."

"You are both doing a great job," Grandpa says proudly as Asmita makes another sale. She sells a pink handbag and matching shoes to a little girl and her mother from their school. "One last tip don't forget to use friendly conversation to attract more customers to your stand," Grandpa reminds the girls.

Walking through the crowds of people Grandpa stops to speak to Matt, Alice and their Mom. "Your handmade cards look wonderful," Grandpa says to Alice, "how is your garage sale going?"

"We've been so busy," Matt tells Grandpa.

"Busier than I thought they would be," Mom comments, "I'm so glad we are organized with our pricing, otherwise we would be a bit confused."

"Yes, it seems that organization is important in a stall like this, you're doing a great job," Grandpa exclaims as Lucy stops to take a photo of Matt and Alice in front of their garage sale.

Following the sound of splashing water Grandpa wanders over to the edge of the

park to speak to Kemba and Leo at the

carwash.

"You still have a line of customers there

Kemba," Grandpa calls over the sound of

the hose washing off a red hatchback.

"We have been super busy all day and I'm soaked," Kemba replies happily, shaking his hands and splashing soap suds on the grass.

"Lucky it's a warm sunny day then," Grandpa points out, "and how about you Leo? How is your dog walking service? Have you taken lots of bookings yet?"

"I haven't had a chance to talk to many people about it," Leo replies, "the car wash is too busy and Kemba needs my help."

"Oh, you're a good friend Leo," Grandpa says admiringly, "hopefully there will be time later for you to take some bookings."

At midday, Grandpa turns down the music being played from the ice cream van and uses the speaker to let everyone know it is time for Jake's magic show.

In a big, showman's voice Grandpa thunders, "Ladies and gentlemen, boys and girls. It is my pleasure to welcome you to our lunchtime entertainment. If you haven't already bought a ticket and would like to watch, see the young lady sitting at the table over there. Now please put your hands together for my grandson, Jake the Magnificent!"

The crowd heads over to the large rotunda in the middle of the park. Jake has set up a stage inside with some seats for his audience, while others stand around the edge. He has a sign for decoration and a table to hold his props. The crowd applauds and Jake starts his first act, a disappearing coin trick.

Chapter 11

What is Success and what to do with it?

After a long busy day, the market has wound down and the customers have all gone home. After packing up their stalls, the kids have come together in front the rotunda and are relaxing on the grass talking with Grandpa about their day.

"Kids, I just want to say what a wonderful market you created," Grandpa exclaims, "you all put so much thought and effort into your businesses, and your customers were very impressed. One measure of how well your business is running is how successful you feel. What does success mean to you and do you think your business was successful?"

"I think our garage sale was successful," Matt says, "we sold a lot of our stuff, with only a few items left. I think that's pretty successful. There's hardly anything to pack back into the car."

"Kemba's car wash was successful," Leo says, "we were busy all day and we ran out of soap. But my dog walking service wasn't. I didn't concentrate on advertising or speaking to people about it, so I didn't get many people to sign their dogs up."

"You didn't concentrate on your business because you were helping me," Kemba says, "because you worked just as hard as me, I'm going to share my profits with you half-half and don't worry I will help you this week to get lots of customers for your dog walking service."

"That is great teamwork Kemba," Grandpa says, "Even though you had everything you needed to be successful, unfortunately you didn't get your chance to accomplish your plan Leo. But with Kemba's help it sounds like you will be fully booked for walks before you know it. What about you

Asmita, I saw how many things you had for sale in your store, did you sell everything?"

"I didn't sell everything, but that's ok because I had already decided anything I didn't sell I would donate to charity. It was Lucy's idea."

"What a wonderful idea girls, that is very socially conscious of you," Grandpa says, "Mei, what about you?"

"Today was hard," Mei responds, "all my customers wanted to do was bargain with me."

"Yes, negotiation is a hard skill to master, like I mentioned before it takes practice," Grandpa says.

"I saw it was easier for Matt and Alice with set prices," Mei notes, thinking that she would have had more time to spend with other customers if she wasn't busy negotiating with the customers who wanted to bargain. "Maybe next time I will have set prices."

"That's a good lesson to learn," Grandpa says, "Another important part of any business is making money. If your business isn't making money you may not feel it's worth your time and effort. Sometimes you need to give it a few goes before you truly know.

Just as importantly is deciding what you are going to do with the money you have made. Kemba has already said he is going to share his profits with Leo for helping him today.

There are three easy ways to use your money. You can 1. spend it, 2. save it for the future or 3. donate it to a good cause.

You could even do some of each. Take the time to think carefully about how you will manage your money.

But first, because you've become kid entrepreneurs and did such a great job today come over to the van. Ice creams for everyone!"

hereshowyoucantoo.com

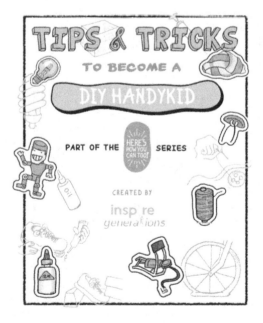

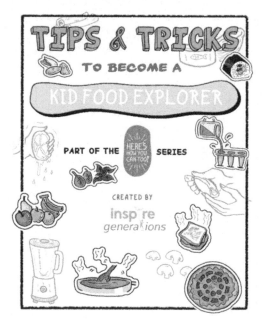

All books available in eBook and print formats.

Please follow us on social media.

Created by

inspire
generations

The Here's How You Can Too! adventure series are fiction story books based on the characters and practical skills introduced in the Here's How You Can Too! picture book and Tips and Tricks series. It is aimed at upper primary school and provides insights into the thoughts, reactions and emotions kids face when developing these skills.

If you liked the book, we would dearly appreciate you supporting us by writing a review. Thank you so much!

About the Author:

Amanda enthusiastically jumped at the opportunity to author the first adventure in the Here's How You Can Too! children's short stories range which aims to provide kids with how-to knowledge and promote a can-do attitude.

She has studied children's literature and loves to create characters that children engage with and will be able to learn alongside. She lives in Sydney, Australia with her partner Jeremy, their son Jonathan and their 'fur-baby' Frank.

Made in the USA
Monee, IL
09 December 2019